STINGRAY

SUBTERRANEAN SEA
BY GRAHAM MARKS

B⬛XTREE

Somewhere deep in the ocean, at an underwater drilling camp, a huge task had just been completed.

'Well, Mr Prescott,' said a white-coated scientist, walking over to his colleague. 'Drilling is complete - we're through the earth's mantle!'

'*Wonderful*, Andrews!' beamed Mr Prescott, looking up from his microscope. 'It's been a long, dangerous job, but we succeeded. Well, come on, don't keep me in suspense - what's beneath the earth's crust?'

'Sea water, Sir. Plain, ordinary sea water!'

'What are you talking about, Andrews?'

'We checked and double-checked, Sir - there's definitely an ocean under the mantle.'

'We spend years drilling through silt and rock to find more sea?'

'Yes, Sir, but it is an important discovery...'

'Important?' said Mr Prescott, standing up. 'Of course it's important - heaven knows what life that sea holds! We've got to find out. Get in contact with the World Aquanaut Security Patrol!'

Just at that moment in a Marineville apartment a suitcase was being zipped up.

'OK,' said Captain Troy Tempest, picking up his sunglasses. 'The packing's done!'

'Yeah, isn't it great to be going on vacation?' replied Phones, relaxing in an easy chair in his white polo-neck and brightly coloured shirt. 'I wonder how the girls are doing?'

'Thank goodness for that - finally closed!' exclaimed Atlanta, snapping shut the case Marina was sitting on, and then looking round at the six other cases that were standing by the door. 'It's a pity we can't take all we wanted, but Troy did say to travel light!'

Back in Troy's apartment, the two friends were just about to leave to pick the girls up when the vid-phone beeped and Commander Shore appeared on the screen.

'Glad you're still there, Troy!'

'We were just about to leave, Sir.'

'Can you come to the control room…it's pretty important.'

'I'll be right there, Commander!'

'Bring the others along, will you?' asked Shore.

'I wonder what he's cooking up?' said Phones, as they left the apartment.

'Probably just wants to wish us *bon voyage*, that's all!' replied Troy, locking the door.

'Ah…there you are,' muttered the Commander, looking up from some papers he was reading. 'I'm cancelling your holiday, Captain!' he growled.

'Cancelling it!? But we're all packed!' Troy couldn't keep the shock out of his voice.

'It's cancelled and that's final!' said the Commander. 'I want you to report to the Undersea Mantle Boring Base at 09.00 hours tomorrow…you'll find out what your mission is when you get there.'

'There's no point in getting mad, Atlanta,' whispered Troy as they walked out to change back into uniform. 'The Commander's made his mind up and I guess that's it…'

Within minutes Troy, Phones and Marina were on board Stingray, ready to launch, and a couple of hours later Phones spotted the base. It was a vast silvery construction, sprawling over the ocean floor below them like a small town.

'Drilling camp from Stingray!' Phones called over the radio. 'Permission to enter.'

'Stingray from drilling camp - proceed!' came back the reply, and a pair of doors, exactly like those at Marineville, opened to admit Stingray.

'Our aim, Captain,' said Mr Prescott, once Troy and the others were seated in his office, 'has been to find out what is beneath the earth's crust.' Pointing to a huge diagram on the wall he continued: 'Yesterday we found out - down there is an ocean.'

'An ocean?! But where do we come in?' asked Troy, a puzzled expression on his face.

'Your job is to explore it - find out how deep it is.' replied Mr Prescott.

'We'd better warn you,' butted in Andrews, 'you'll be completely on your own. We have no idea of the dangers you may encounter. We've been taking soundings, but for some reason radio waves don't travel down there.'

'OK,' sighed Troy. 'When do we start?'

'Any time you're ready!' Mr Prescott stood up. 'An elevator will take you and your craft down through the two miles of crust to the subterranean ocean.'

Moments later the massive elevator started its incredible journey towards the centre of the earth. 'Huh! Instead of basking in the sun, we're getting further away from it!' snorted Phones.

Further and further down they went, deeper into the earth's crust. The only thing that changed were the figures on the depth gauge, as mile upon mile was notched up.

'We've reached the subterranean sea at last!' cried Troy, as the elevator settled the sub into the gently lapping water. 'Check rear hydroplanes, Phones! Give me acceleration rate 1, and dive - we're off into the unknown!'

'Sure is dark, Troy.' muttered Phones, as they sank beneath the inky waters.

'We're deeper than any craft has ever gone!' said Troy. 'The meters just can't register it - the instruments have gone crazy. OK, let's go deeper!'

As they dived, suddenly the dark sea was lit up with dazzling brightness. 'That light!' Phones shouted, shielding his eyes from a sudden red glare. 'It's blinding!'

'Those rocks!' squinted Troy, putting on his sunglasses. 'They seem to be made from some sort of glass.'

'Yeah…they're kinda fluorescent!' replied Phones as they watched an ever-changing procession of intensely glowing rocks - red and blue, green and yellow.

'What fantastic colours!' said a wide-eyed Troy.

'Say, Troy...' asked Phones as they were watching the weird rock formations. 'Have you noticed anything about the seaweed?'

'Yeah, it all leans in one direction - the one we're going in! There must be a pretty strong current down here!'

'You can say that again!' commented Phones as he watched a large clump of weed being ripped out by its roots and fly past them.

'We're picking up speed, Phones!' warned Troy, as Stingray's nose tipped further down. 'We're going faster still - help me slow her down!!'

'I can't hold her!' yelled Phones, as he watched the instrument panel lights flash madly in front of him. 'She's not responding to the controls!'

'And we're going even deeper!' shouted Troy above the whine of the engine in full reverse-thrust. 'Look out for those rocks!!'

But there was nothing anyone could do. Stingray hit the bottom with a sickening thud and rolled over twice before coming to a halt.

For a moment the only sound that could be heard in the sub was the hiss of the air supply unit. Marina lay on the floor by the table. Troy and Phones were slumped across the controls. Nobody moved. Then...

'What on earth happened?' mumbled Troy as he slowly came to. 'Oh yeah...I remember! We lost control...And, and then the crash...

'Are you OK, Marina?' he asked as he saw her sit up. She nodded.

'Wow! What hit us?' groaned Phones as he came round.

'I don't know, it was like some kind of underwater tidal wave!' said Troy. 'Stingray seems to be OK though - try the motors, Phones.'

'Sure, Troy.' replied his co-pilot, switching on the turbine. But all they could hear was a high-pitched whine.

'I don't get it, Phones...' frowned Troy, listening to the banshee howl of the engine as he walked to the the window. 'All systems are green, but it sounds as if we're running in the dry. Great heavens! The water's gone!!'

'Let's get out there and take a look. We'd better put on our skin suits and breathing gear,' ordered Troy. 'We want to be prepared for anything - there's no water at the moment and I doubt that there's any air down here, so give Marina a mask as well.'

Soon they were climbing out of Stingray - ready to explore. Everywhere they looked there were strange plants, and the 'sky' was a deep purple colour. Crystals the size of large boulders littered the ground, and here and there the sand bubbled as the three intrepid adventurers went where no human had ever set foot.

'I don't get this!' said Troy. 'One minute this is an ocean, the next it becomes a desert - is this a crazy dream Phones?'

'Sure feels like one!'

As they walked off, a brilliant green lizard looked out from beneath a rock, one of a thousand pairs of eyes that were watching them...

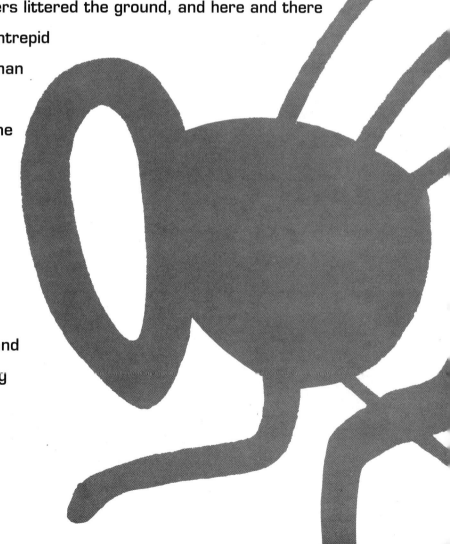

'Look at those rocks!' gasped Troy as they walked. 'They must be red-hot!'

'Yeah! My feet are sizzling as well!' joked Phones. 'You could fry eggs on the soles of my shoes!'

'Say! This must be pretty close to the centre of the earth - no wonder it's hot!'

Suddenly Marina stopped to listen, her ultra-sensitive hearing picking up something unusual.

'Phones! Marina's heard something. Stop and listen!'

'I can't hear a thing, Troy!'

'Wait! I hear it now - that roaring sound again!' Troy turned back. 'It's the water! Come on - back to Stingray... and fast!'

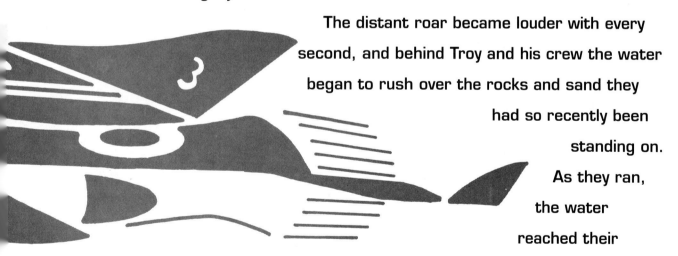

The distant roar became louder with every second, and behind Troy and his crew the water began to rush over the rocks and sand they had so recently been standing on. As they ran, the water reached their ankles...then it was swirling round their knees...in mere seconds it was up above their waists. And somewhere, not far behind, a great wall of water was bearing down upon them...

The water was now deep enough to lift their feet off the ground, and the current was so strong that they couldn't fight it.

'Swim as hard as you can!' Troy yelled, as a surge of water almost flung the three of them past Stingray. But they all managed to get aboard without harm.

'Start the engine, Phones - and hold her steady!' ordered Troy as soon as they were back in their seats. Fighting with the controls, they managed to bring the sub off the ocean floor.

'What was that all about, Troy?'

'I can only think that this sea has tides just like any other.' pondered Troy. 'Only down here it's a flood tide every time, and the heat from the centre of the earth dries the bed out almost instantly! Now, set a course for that elevator shaft Phones!'

'I can't!' cried Phones. 'All the instruments have been shattered!'

'See if the sound-scanner is working - it's our last hope!'

'We're in luck, Troy!' cried Phones. 'But the scanner's only showing the impulses bouncing off the bottom of the earth's crust!'

'Keep at it,' frowned Troy. 'We've got to find that shaft!'

With every minute that passed, the air gauge fell, registering almost empty...

'Three hours with the same pattern on the screen!' sighed Phones.

'Keep trying.' They were feeling faint; Marina was almost unconscious. As Troy searched the rock formations for the shaft he suddenly heard the sound-scanner's impulse change in tone.

'It's an opening, Troy!' yelled Phones. 'It must be the shaft!'

'No, it's a different one, but we'll have to take a chance!' said Troy through gritted teeth. 'Stand by to surface - blow the tanks!'

Stingray powered up through a narrow tunnel for miles and miles, until finally a light could be seen and, just in time, the sub broke the surface of an idyllic tropical lagoon.

'What a beautiful island!' smiled Troy, as he relaxed on the beach later, listening to Marina play guitar as an islander danced to the music.

'Looks like we got our vacation after all!'

'We sure did - although poor old Atlanta's still stuck in the office!'

First published in the UK 1992 by BOXTREE LTD, Broadwall House, 21 Broadwall,
London SE1 9PL
1 3 5 7 9 10 8 6 4 2
Copyright © 1992 ITC ENTERTAINMENT GROUP LTD.
Licensed by Copyright Promotions Ltd.
Design and illustrations by Arkadia
1-85283-775-6
Printed and bound in Great Britain by Lawrence Allen, Weston-super-Mare
A catalogue record for this book is available from the British Library

Caring
for Orphans

Published by Ali Gator Productions
Copyright © 2017 Ali Gator Productions, Second Edition,
First Published 2016

National Library of Australia Cataloguing–in-Publication (CIP) data:
Vani Diana P., Caring for Orphans
ISBN: 978-1-921772-36-8
For primary school age, Juvenile fiction, Dewey Number: 823.92

Adopted from the original title Sayang Anak Yatim first published by Dar! Mizan.
Copyright © 2009 by Author Vani Diana P., Illustrator Studio Air. Printed in Indonesia.

T: +61 (3) 9386 2771 F: +61 (3) 9478 8854
P.O. Box 2536, Regent West, Melbourne Victoria, 3072 Australia
E: info@ali-gator.com W: www.ali-gator.com

▬   ▬   ▬   ▬   ▬

The aim of the Akhlaaq Building for Kids Series is to inspire young children to develop good Akhlaaq (manners) through fun stories involving young children like themselves.

The main characters are a young girl Saaliha and her younger brother Ali.

Along with their friends they experience various situations, all with a moral message for the young readers.

In Sha Allah (God Willing) if this series helps to inspire our young readers to be better people, following the best of example in manners and behavior, the Prophet Muhammad (peace be upon him), then we have truly achieved our goal.

BISMILLAHIR RAHMANIR RAHIM
IN THE NAME OF ALLAH, MOST GRACIOUS, MOST MERCIFUL

4

One day Saaliha and Ali's mother decided to take her children to visit the orphans.

When they arrived at the orphanage they were welcomed by Mrs Marwa.

"Would you like to visit our babies?" she asked.

"Yes please," replied an excited Saaliha and Ali.

Mrs Marwa took Saaliha and Ali and their mother to a large room.

There were several playpens with babies inside. Some were drinking milk, some were sleeping and some were playing with the nurses.

"They are all so cute," commented Saaliha.

6

7

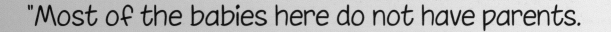

"Most of the babies here do not have parents.

Or those that do have parents find it very hard to raise their children.

They are so poor they can't afford to buy them milk or food," explained Mrs Marwa.

"That's so sad," said Saaliha with a tear in her eye.

Saaliha and Ali both decided that they were going
to do whatever they could to help these orphans.

So they played lots of games with them.
They all had a great time together,
which now made Saaliha very happy.

Ali decided to play dress ups and pretended to be in a marching parade.

Saaliha and the little orphans all followed Ali around laughing as they marched up and down.

Everyone was so happy that Saaliha and Ali had come to visit them.

13

Saaliha and Ali treated the orphans just like all their other friends.

They never mocked or insulted them. They remembered that their father had told them that the Prophet Muhammad (pbuh) was an orphan, and that we should treat everyone the same.

PBUH
PEACE BE UPON HIM

15

When they got home from the orphanage,
Saaliha told her mother,
"I would like to give away my baby clothes
to the children at the orphanage."

"That's a great idea Saaliha,"
said her proud mother.

"I also want to give away mine," added Ali,
who never wants to miss out
on doing anything.

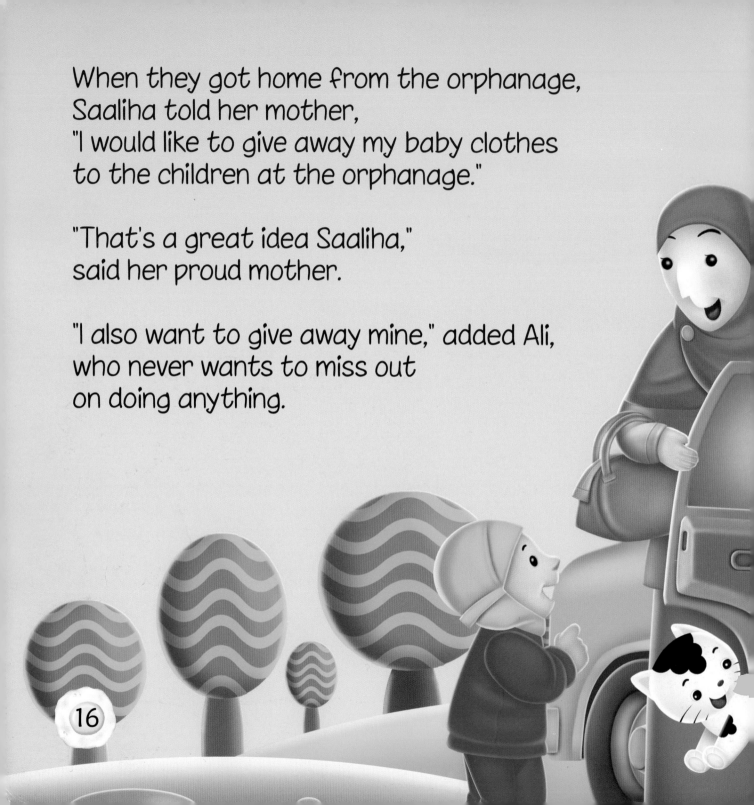

So Saaliha and Ali went through their old baby clothes and toys to see which ones were of good quality to give to the orphans.

Then, they wrapped them neatly and gave them to their mother.

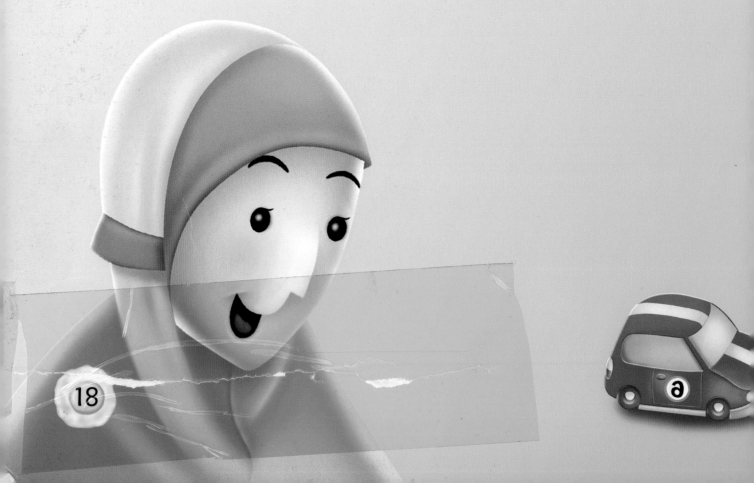

19

Saaliha and Ali's parents were both very proud of how their children helped the orphans.

"Allah loves those that help others," reminded their mother.

This made Saaliha and Ali very happy.

Because Saaliha and Ali went to visit the orphans, they now have more new friends.

They like to share their clothes and their toys with their new friends. But best of all they love to play games all together.

ALHAMDULILLAH
PRAISE BE TO ALLAH